NICKELODEON

Drake & Josh

Josh Is Done

NICKELODEON®

Drake & Josh™

Josh Is Done

Adapted by Laurie McElroy
Based on "I Love Sushi," written by Dan Schneider
and "Josh Is Done," written by Ethan Banville

Based on *Drake & Josh* created by Dan Schneider

SCHOLASTIC INC.
New York Toronto London Auckland Sydney
Mexico City New Delhi Hong Kong Buenos Aires

ISBN-13: 978-0-439-91647-9

ISBN-10: 0-439-91647-X

Published by Scholastic Inc. SCHOLASTIC and associated logos are trademarks and/or registered trademarks of Scholastic Inc.

12 11 10 9 8 7 6 5 4 3 8 9 10/0

Printed in the U.S.A.
First printing, December 2007

NICKELODEON

Drake & Josh

Josh Is Done

Part One:
I Love Sushi

Prologue

Drake Parker was in the kitchen, rearranging his stepfather's hat collection.

Who collects hats, he wondered? And what were they doing in the kitchen? He put a 1940's fedora on top of a watermelon and stood back to admire his work. "You know what?" he asked.

Josh Nichols was in his bedroom, performing a painful monthly grooming ritual. He yanked out a nose hair and blinked away the tears that suddenly filled his eyes. If he didn't do this

himself, he knew his sister Megan would do it for him — when he was least expecting it. "You know what?" he asked.

"I've been noticing," Drake said, substituting an old-fashioned black leather motorcycle cap for the fedora.

"There's a pattern in my life," Josh said, screwing up the courage to tackle another nose hair.

"Whenever Josh gets me involved in something," Drake said, pausing to try another hat on the melon.

"Every time Drake drags me into one of his little adventures . . ." Josh said.

"Things go bad," Drake finished, not knowing that his brother was saying the same exact thing in another room.

"Things go bad," Josh said, at the same exact time as Drake.

"Bad," Drake said again, for emphasis.

"Bad." Josh repeated, yanking out another nose hair and pressing a finger against his sore nostril.

Drake blinked in surprise. "You know what I mean?" he asked, sliding a pirate's hat onto the watermelon.

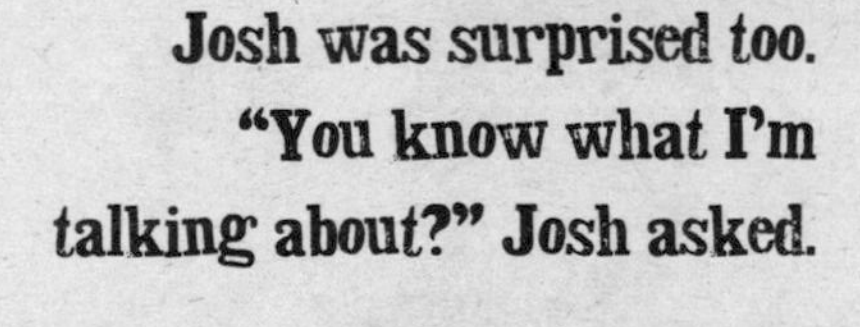

Josh was surprised *too*. "You know what I'm talking about?" Josh asked.

"You do?" Drake asked again, totally confused. Since when did anyone agree with him?

"Oh, you do," Josh said. He was all ready to rant and rave about Drake and his crazy adventures, but there was no reason to now.

"Well . . . okay," Drake said. Did that mean he had to stop complaining about Josh now? Complaining about Josh was one of his favorite things to do.

"Then I guess I've made my point," Josh said in a disappointed tone. He didn't have much to say if he wasn't complaining about Drake.

"I was gonna tell you a little story . . ." Drake said.

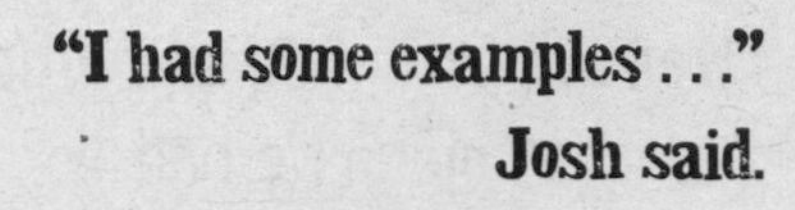

"I had some examples . . ." Josh said.

"... about Josh, you know, being annoying," Drake finished. He had so many stories to choose from — like the time they waited in line for hours to ride an awesome new roller coaster. Then Josh got into a fight with a little kid and with the theme park's mascot, and both brothers got thrown to the back of the line — twice!

". . . about Drake and his irritating ways," Josh said, completing his thought. He had wanted to tell about the time that Drake talked him into pretending to be Drake's chauffeur, and Josh ended up with two traffic tickets!

"But if you already get it," Drake said with a sigh. "I guess I'm done."

"But if you already know what I mean," Josh said, his voice trailing off. "Have a nice day."

CHAPTER ONE

Josh Nichols stood behind the snack counter at the Premiere, a local movie theater and café where lots of his friends hung out. Josh worked there after school and on weekends, wearing the red vest with the giant P on the lapel that all the Premiere employees wore. He handed an extra large bucket of popcorn to a customer with a smile. "Enjoy your movie," he said.

His stepbrother, Drake Parker, walked in with a pretty girl Josh recognized from school. Her name was Lucy, he remembered.

"Hey, what's up?" Josh asked.

"We're gonna see a movie," Drake answered.

"Cool. Do you want some snacks?"

"I like pancakes," Lucy said with a big smile.

Josh stared at her for a second, waiting for a punch line. But she was serious. The girl was actually asking for pancakes in a movie theater. Hello, had she ever been to a movie before? He eyed his brother.

Drake only shrugged. What could he do? The girl liked pancakes.

"Okay, um, but this is a movie theater, so how about some popcorn?" Josh asked.

"Okay," Lucy answered, her smile even bigger now.

Josh handed her an extra large bucket and then watched her pull a bottle of maple syrup out of her bag. Lucy turned the bottle upside down and started to squeeze, pouring syrup all over the popcorn.

Drake looked away. He knew if he caught Josh's eye he would totally crack up. This girl didn't just like pancakes, she was obsessed with them — or with the syrup that normally went on top of them.

Josh cringed, watching her drown the popcorn in syrup. It looked totally gross. "You carry around a bottle of syrup with you?" he asked.

"Uh, yeah," Lucy answered with a confused expression. She looked at Drake and shook her head over the silliness of Josh's question. Didn't everybody carry syrup around with them?

"Don't your hands get all sticky?" Josh asked.

"Uh huh," she answered cheerfully.

Drake grimaced. There would definitely be no holding hands with this girl — and he wasn't going to eat any of that syrupy popcorn either. "Why don't you go save us two seats," he said.

"Okay," Lucy agreed, walking toward the theater. She had no idea that Drake was about to ask for Josh's help in ditching her and her syrup — and fast.

But just then, one of Josh's colleagues on the Premiere staff ran over. "Hey Josh, did you sign up?" Leah asked, breathless with excitement.

"Sign up for what?" Josh asked.

"See those two people over there?" she asked, pointing to a man and a woman standing behind a table. A small group of kids was gathered around them, filling out forms on clipboards. "They're producers from *Pump My Room*."

Drake's eyes lit up. He didn't know for sure what *Pump My Room* was, but it sounded like a television show and it sounded cool. "C'mon, let's go sign up," he said.

"Well, what about your date?" Josh asked.

"Oh, she's fine," Drake answered, waving off Josh's concern. "She's got popcorn and syrup. C'mon," he urged, pushing Josh toward the table.

"Excuse me," Josh asked. "Is this where we sign up?"

"Sure," the guy said.

"How's it work?" Drake asked.

The woman stepped forward with a clipboard. "You just fill out this form," she said, handing it to Josh with an eager smile. "Then you go home, make a video presentation showing us your room and telling us why you deserve to have it pumped." She pumped both fists in the air for emphasis.

Her enthusiasm was contagious. Drake tapped Josh on the shoulder. "We have a room," he said.

"And we deserve to have it pumped," Josh agreed, pumping his fist in the air.

The guy in the suit handed Josh a pen. "Give it a shot!"

The brothers bent over the clipboard, all their attention focused on filling out the form perfectly — until Lucy came out of the movie theater.

"Umm." She held her hands up with an embarrassed giggle. It looked like she was wearing popcorn gloves — the sticky syrup had practically glued the popcorn to her hands. "Where's the little girl's room?"

Josh looked at his brother. Where did he find these girls? "Yeah, she's a good one," he said.

Drake rolled his eyes and turned back to the form — popcorn hands was on her own.

CHAPTER TWO

Drake and Josh raced home as soon as Josh got off of work and headed upstairs to the bedroom they shared.

"Okay, get the camcorder," Drake said, looking around at their room. He imagined it totally pumped.

"Getting it," Josh said, jumping onto his bed and running across it to the closet on the other side. Walking around it would have taken too much time.

"Man, do you realize how awesome it will be if we actually win this room makeover?" Drake asked.

Josh found the camcorder in the back of the closet. "Uh, very," he agreed. "Hey, you know what this room needs?"

"Yeah," Drake said, picturing the perfect room. He knew exactly where to put things too. He pointed as he listed his wishes. "A hot tub, a hammock, and a vibrating chair."

"Or, a vibrating couch," Josh said, getting into the spirit of the fantasy.

"Better," Drake agreed with a nod.

The guys hadn't always seen eye to eye on what their room should look like or even whether they could live in it together. The bedroom they shared used to be Drake's private paradise. But when Drake's mom married Josh's dad, the guys suddenly became brothers and roommates.

The room stretched from the front of the house to the back, over the garage. It was unfinished, with exposed beams and unpainted wallboards. Drake liked it that way. He had built a loft bed under the window, bought an old couch and a couple of chairs at yard sales, and filled the walls with posters, road signs, and old license plates. It was a pretty cool room, and it was certainly big enough for two guys.

But just because the room was big enough for two didn't mean Drake was exactly happy about sharing it at first. He was totally into having a good time — playing his guitar and hanging with his friends. He wasn't big on school — well, except for the girls — and he'd rather do anything than homework.

Josh, on the other hand, was totally into following the rules. Not only did he do all his homework and study for tests, he actually liked school. He didn't hang with the same high school in-crowd as Drake did.

Josh was completely excited about being Drake's brother. Drake wasn't so sure at first. But eventually, they found some things in common. Now they were more than brothers — they were best friends too. They liked nothing better than kicking back on the couch, feet up on the coffee table, listening to tunes, watching the tube, or playing video games. But having their room pumped would be totally amazing.

Josh sat on the couch. It was time to come up with a plan. "If we're going to win this thing we have to make sure this video is totally awesome."

Their younger sister Megan opened the door and breezed in, completely ignoring her brothers as she headed for Josh's desk. Megan was even less thrilled than Drake was by the idea of having a new brother. At first she thought being outnumbered by the guys would put her at a disadvantage, but Megan quickly learned that she was much better at pranks than either Drake or Josh. One of her favorite hobbies was coming up with devious pranks to mess with her brothers. She had become an expert.

Josh stared at her. "Hey, you know you could knock," he said, sarcastically.

Megan flipped her long black hair over her shoulder and started going through Josh's desk drawer. "Yeah, and you could have a normal sized head," she answered. "But you don't, do you?"

Josh looked at Drake for support.

Drake shook his head and shrugged his shoulders. "You don't," he said apologetically.

"Can we help you?" Josh asked Megan, totally frustrated. His tone made it clear that he didn't like Megan going through his things, but he knew Megan didn't care.

She had found what she was looking for. "I just need to borrow your hot glue gun," she said.

"Ahhhh," Drake groaned. He didn't pay attention in math, but he knew that Megan plus hot glue plus gun equaled trouble. He rushed toward her, holding his hands out in front of himself for protection. "Hot glue gun. You. I don't like it," he said, eyeing her suspiciously.

"Relax," Megan said. "I'm just making a present for Mom and Dad's anniversary."

"Isn't that like two weeks away?" Josh asked.

"Yeah, why are you making it now?" Drake added, even more suspicious.

"Cuz, I'm a busy person," Megan explained. She listed all the things she had to do. "Between school, oboe practice, gymnastics, and collecting antique sponges, I barely have time to breathe."

"Well, feel free to stop breathing anytime," Drake said with a laugh.

Megan glared at him.

Drake realized that insulting Megan while she was holding a hot glue gun in her hand wasn't the smartest thing he had ever done. So he tried to blame it on Josh. "He said it," Drake said, pointing at his brother.

Josh stared at Drake. "No I didn't," he said, outraged. He did not need Megan to find another excuse to prank him. Last time, his underwear had shown up all over the Internet.

Megan rolled her eyes, but really, she liked the fact that her brothers were a little afraid of her. "I'm leaving," she said, heading out of the room.

"When you're done with that glue gun, make sure you bring it back," Josh said. Now that his sister was safely across the room, he was brave enough to let her know he was tired of her taking his things and not returning them.

"No," Megan said over her shoulder.

"All right then," Josh said lamely. There really wasn't anything he could do. Megan got the better of him every time.

Drake shook his head — they had more important things to think about than Megan. "All right, c'mon," he said. "Let's just focus on making an awesome tape so that we win that room makeover." Maybe the producers of *Pump Your Room* would come up with a booby-trapped door that would keep Megan out. Their room would finally be a completely safe place — a Megan-free zone.

But Megan had given Josh another idea. "Hey, what if we try to win the makeover for Mom and Dad?" he asked.

"Why?" Drake asked, totally confused. Who cared about what their parents' room looked like?

"For their anniversary," Josh explained. "If we win, we could have them make over the living room. Don't you think that would be really nice?"

Drake shrugged. He'd rather have a hot tub and a hammock. "We always get them something really nice."

Really nice? Was Drake serious? "Last year you gave them a coupon book," Josh said. "That you found in a Dumpster."

"Yeah, Walter got forty percent off a shovel, and mom got two salamis for the price of one," Drake said.

"Yup. Nothing says happy anniversary like two salamis and a shovel," Josh said sarcastically.

Drake didn't get the sarcasm. He threw his arms up in the air. "That's what I'm saying!"

"C'mon, it's their fifth anniversary," Josh said, grabbing the tripod for the camera.

Drake sighed. He knew that once Josh got an idea like this into his head there was no way of talking him out of it. "All right," he agreed reluctantly. "We'll try to win the room makeover for mom and Walter."

Josh put his hand on Drake's shoulder with a smile. He was about to say something nice, but Megan shouted from across the hall.

"Okay, you can have your hot glue gun back."

The brothers eyed each other. They'd better take cover. Drake slammed the bedroom door just in time.

Thwack!

Slowly and carefully they opened their bedroom door. The hot glue gun was stuck to the door, pointed end first. Luckily, it had just hit the door and not one of their foreheads.

Drake jiggled the gun. It wasn't budging — it was going to be attached to their door forever — like a bizarre doorknocker. "Quality glue," he said finally.

"Yup," Josh said, relieved and grateful he wouldn't have to walk around with a glue gun on his forehead for the rest of his life.

CHAPTER THREE

Drake and Josh sat on the couch in the living room. After writing a script and having two rehearsals, they were ready to shoot their video. The camera was set up on a tripod in front of them.

Josh clicked a button on the remote and the red light on the camera began to blink. "Dear *Pump My Room*," he said, with a huge smile. Then he spread his arms out wide. "This is our living room."

Drake's smile was just as big as Josh's, and his words were just as stiff and awkward. "The room in which we live."

Josh leaned forward. "We really hope we win this makeover," he said earnestly.

"But not for us," Drake said.

Josh nodded. "For our parents."

"We call them Mom and Dad," Drake said, folding his hands together as if he was praying.

Josh made the same rehearsed hand movement, and nodded along with Drake. "You see," Josh explained. "My dad married his mom almost five years ago."

"I am still in shock," Drake said. He pointed to his face. His jaw dropped in fake surprise.

Josh nodded again. "And soon, it'll be their fifth anniversary."

Drake pointed to his face again. "Still in shock."

"Now we can't afford to buy them anything fancy," Josh said.

"So we pray that you wonderful people at *Pump My Room* choose us," Drake said, folding his hands in prayer-mode again.

"Nay," Josh said, holding up his finger. "Our parents."

"For the special gift of a room makeover," Drake added. He paused dramatically, and then gave the camera his most heartfelt expression while he clasped his hands under his chin. "Please."

Josh pretended to be near tears while he nodded along with Drake. "Please," he said.

The brothers turned to each other and leaned into a hug, both of them totally pretending to be overcome with emotion. Drake clicked the button on the remote and they jumped to their feet.

"All right, good one. Good one," Josh said, rubbing his hands together. But was it enough? Had they shown enough emotion? "I still think one of us needs to cry," he said.

"All right," Drake said. "I'll punch you in the stomach and we'll do it again." He put one hand on Josh's shoulder and drew the other one back into a fist.

That wasn't exactly what Josh had in mind. He didn't think they needed real pain, just a few tears. "You're gonna punch —" The doorbell rang, saving him from intense pain. "Oh, I'll get it!" he said, running toward the door.

Drake was right behind him, but Josh got there first. He opened the door to find a little kid standing there, with a plate in his hand.

"Hot nachos for Drake and Josh," the kid said.

"We didn't order any —"

Drake cut him off. Was Josh turning down snacks? "Yeah, it's about time our nachos got here," he said.

"But we didn't order any," Josh said again.

"Shhh! Free nachos," Drake said under his breath. He turned back to the boy and grabbed the plate. "I'll take those. Josh, tip the nacho boy."

Josh was still confused, but he pulled his wallet out of his pocket and fumbled with it, trying to get it open. "Do you have change for a five?" he asked, holding out the bill.

The boy took it, and then shook his head with a smile. "No, sir."

Josh watched open-mouthed as the boy turned around and left with Josh's five-dollar bill in his hand.

Drake was already digging in.

"We didn't order those," Josh repeated, walking over to him.

It was time to teach Josh an important life lesson. "Dude, when life hands you free nachos, you don't question it," Drake said, taking another bite.

"I just worry about who really did order them," Josh said. He checked out the plate in Drake's hand. There was just the right amount of melted cheese over the nachos, and generous scoops of salsa and sour cream in the middle of the salty chips, just the way Josh liked them. He grabbed one and took a bite. "Oh my gosh, these are good nachos."

"Seriously," Drake said, shoving another chip in his mouth.

"These are the best nachos in the world," Josh said, stuffing his mouth full.

"They're made with like five different kinds of cheeses," Drake said, sitting down on the couch. It was hard to form the words with his mouth full of chips and salsa.

"What'd you say?" Josh asked. But his mouth was full too, and it was hard to get his lips and tongue to say the words. "How many different kinds of cheeses?"

Drake tried to answer, but he couldn't get the words out. His mouth wasn't doing what it was supposed to do. "It's getting kind of hard for me to swallow," he said, sounding like he had just had about fifty shots of Novocain at the dentist's office.

Neither brother noticed Megan and the delivery boy crouched down in the kitchen, peering at Drake and Josh through the pass-through window. They were trying hard not to crack up.

"Something's wrong with these nachos," Josh said. He sounded just as bad as Drake. It was like his tongue was suddenly too big for his mouth. He didn't seem to be able to swallow the food in his mouth, but he couldn't open up his lips wide enough to spit it out either.

Megan and the delivery boy walked into the room. "Awesome," Megan said, applauding. "Great, great work."

"You really think so?" the boy asked, wide-eyed. Megan was the prank expert, and she just said he had done great work!

Megan nodded, and then cocked her eyebrows at her brothers.

Josh tried to yell at her. Drake did too. But neither one of them could do more than grunt and moan.

Megan cut them off. "Drake. Josh. I'd like you to meet my new assistant, Tyler," she said. She turned to Tyler. "Tyler, you know the idiots." It was her favorite name for her brothers. She used it all the time.

Tyler nodded. "Idiots," he said.

Drake and Josh pointed, grunted, and groaned some more. Clearly they were totally outraged.

"I'll explain," Megan said, shushing them again. "See, like I told you, I've been really busy lately. So I don't have time to harass you guys as much as I'd like to." Megan was enjoying the fact that her brothers couldn't speak. She actually got to finish what she wanted to say. "Which is why I hired Tyler as my assistant," she continued. "To help make your lives as miserable as possible."

Drake and Josh stared at each other in disbelief and then turned back to Megan.

"He made the nachos," Megan said, pointing to Tyler.

"I used a special sticky cheese," Tyler said proudly.

"Sticky cheese?" Drake asked, but the words sounded more like "Stinky chis?"

"Yup," Megan said happily. She was obviously pleased with her new employee. "Tyler, come upstairs with me and we'll make a schedule for the rest of the week."

"Yes ma'am," Tyler agreed.

The brothers watched the two of them head for the stairs and Megan's room. But they couldn't open up their mouths to protest. They grunted and moaned and growled, but no actual words came out.

The phone rang. Drake picked it up. "Huwwoo," he said. "No, huwwooo. Yeah, I know, I have a mouf —"

Josh tried to tell Drake to hang up the phone. There was no use trying to talk, their mouths had been sealed shut with sticky cheese.

But Drake thought Josh was trying to criticize. "I'm trying," he said from between his sticky lips, pointing to his mouth.

Josh growled again. He tried to say, "Just hang up," but the words wouldn't come.

"All right, here," Drake grunted, pushing the phone into Josh's hands.

That was the last thing Josh wanted. "Huwwooo?"

"Who is it?" Drake asked.

"Huwwoo," Josh said again, totally frustrated. Then he clicked the phone off and threw it onto the couch.

Whatever this sticky cheese was made of, he hoped it wore off fast.

CHAPTER FOUR

After at least ten cups of hot water with lemon, the sticky cheese was history. By the next day, Drake and Josh had forgotten all about Megan and her new assistant. Josh was working his usual shift at the Premiere, and Drake was just hanging out with him, drinking a mocha cola. They played the "Would You?" game, daring each other with more and more bizarre questions while Josh cleaned the counter.

"Okay, your turn. Go," Drake said.

"Okay, um . . ." Josh said, thinking. "All right, here's a good one. If you could be a girl for a whole day, would you do it?"

"Absolutely!" Drake said. He didn't even have to think about that one. As much as he liked girls, they were a total mystery to him. He'd love to figure out why they did the things they did.

"I know, right?" Josh said.

"Yeah," Drake agreed.

Josh's colleague Leah came running in, even more excited than she was the other day. She could hardly get the words out, and sticky cheese had nothing to do with it. "Drake. Josh," she said, turning from one to the other. "The producers from that show *Pump My Room* are looking for you guys!"

"No way!" Josh said.

"What?" Drake asked, dropping his soda.

"Yeah," Leah said, her voice rising in excitement. "They're right over there!"

Josh slammed into Leah, spinning her around as he ran toward the producers. Then Drake knocked into her too, sending her spinning the other way. But the brothers were totally oblivious. They stood in front of the producers, Mark and Maya, babbling excitedly.

"Drake and Josh. Drake and Josh," Josh said to them, pointing from himself to his brother and back again.

"Yeah. Yeah," Drake added, nodding his head.

"All right. Drake Parker and Josh Nichols," the guy said.

"Congratulations," Maya added.

Mark smiled at them. "We loved your video."

"So you've been selected to have your house featured on *Pump My Room*." Maya pumped her fists in the air.

"Yeah," Drake and Josh squealed at the same time, but they were so excited that they sounded like little girls.

Mark laughed. "So here's the deal," he said, putting his arm around Josh. "This Saturday you've got to make sure that everyone is out of your house from eleven A.M. to five P.M."

"Just leave a key under the mat," Maya said.

"We don't have a mat," Josh explained.

"Buy a mat," Maya said. "Leave a key under it. And the *Pump My Room* crew will come in and make sure that your mom and dad's living room is the most special living room in all of San Diego."

"*Awwww*," Drake and Josh said at the same time.

"This is so great," Josh said. He didn't even know how to say thank you. This was the best present he and Josh would ever be able to give to their parents.

"Well, I think you're going to be very pleased when you get home on Saturday," Mark said, shaking Drake's hand.

Maya shook hands with Josh, then the four of them formed an "X" while Maya shook Drake's hand and Mark reached for Josh's.

"Oh, I can't believe it!" Josh said to his brother as soon as the producers left.

"I know!" Drake answered. "I've got to do something!" He ran around the Premiere, hugging everyone he saw. Then he remembered — he had to buy a mat! He ran out the door, waving to Josh over his shoulder.

On Saturday, Drake and Josh kept their parents out of the house all day, making up one excuse after another. To be extra sure the *Pump Your Room* people had time to give their parents the coolest living room in San Diego, they wouldn't let Audrey and Walter Nichols near the house until an hour after Mark and Maya said they would be finished.

Josh could hardly contain his excitement as he walked up the front walk. This was going to be his parents' best anniversary gift of all time. "Okay, Mom and Dad, here it comes," he said, stopping in front of the door.

Drake ran and stood next to him. "Who's ready to go inside?" he asked.

Their excitement was contagious. Audrey Nichols started to laugh. "What is up with you guys?"

"Yeah. You kept us out all day," Mr. Nichols added. "Driving all over the city."

"What's going on? " Mrs. Nichols asked.

"Get ready," Drake said with a grin, opening the front door. He walked into the dark house, followed by Josh.

Drake reached for the light switch and together the brothers got ready to surprise their parents. "Happy Annivers —"

The guys stopped mid-word when the lights came on and illuminated an empty room — a totally empty room. The *Pump My Room* guys hadn't given the Nichols the best new living room in San Diego. They had stolen every single thing out of the old one — even the dust bunnies were missing.

"— sary," the guys finished lamely.

"Drake?" Mr. Nichols said.

Mrs. Nichols gasped. "Josh?"

"Where's our stuff?" they asked together.

"We've been robbed!" Josh yelled.

"Surprise," Drake said, trying to figure out how things could have gone so wrong — so horribly and completely wrong.

CHAPTER FIVE

An hour later, Walter Nichols sat on the floor in the middle of his empty living room and his empty house while Drake and Josh talked to two police officers.

Megan came home from oboe practice, slamming the front door behind her. Her eyes widened, when instead of a couch and a television and lamps and a rug, all she saw were four walls and a bare floor. "What happened?" she asked her father.

Mr. Nichols looked up at her sadly. "Drake and Josh let bad people steal our stuff," he explained.

Megan sat down next to him and watched her mother walk to the kitchen's pass-through window with a can of coffee in her hand. "Sergeant Doty," she said.

One of the police officers turned to her.

"I have coffee, but I can't make it because they stole our coffee maker," she said.

Sergeant Doty needed his caffeine fix to get through this case, coffee maker or no coffee maker.

"Just bring me the dry coffee with a spoon," he said. He turned back to the guys, paging through his notebook. "So, let me see if I've got this straight," he said.

"Sure," Josh said.

"Go ahead," Drake added.

"You two supposedly won a home makeover from some TV show you never heard of."

"That's right," Josh said quietly.

Drake nodded in agreement. "Yeah."

"And at their request you made sure that no one was at home today for six hours," Sergeant Doty continued.

"Right," Josh said, nodding. He was still kind of proud about what they had tried to do for their parents.

"That's pretty much it," Drake added.

"So what do you guys think?" Josh asked with a smile.

"I think you're idiots," Sergeant Doty said.

Megan had been listening. "We know they're idiots," she said, getting up and walking over to the group. Her father followed, still more than a little confused.

Mrs. Nichols walked in with the can of dry coffee and a spoon. The thieves had stolen their silverware, but she found an old plastic spoon with the picnic supplies in the garage.

"So, do you think you can get our furniture back?" Mr. Nichols asked.

The police officer chewed on a heaping spoonful of dry coffee. "I don't know," he said. Then he turned the coffee can around to read the label. "Good coffee," he said.

"Thank you," Audrey Nichols said with a grimace. She had never seen anyone eat something quite so disgusting.

"Man, I can't believe they took everything," Megan said, looking around.

"I need an aspirin." Walter Nichols rubbed his forehead and headed for his bedroom.

"I'll bring you some juice," Mrs. Nichols said.

"Pineapple," Mr. Nichols said over his shoulder.

"I'll bring him the juice," Megan offered.

"*Awww*, thanks sweetie," Mrs. Nichols said, following her husband.

But Megan had gotten what she wanted — points

from her mom. "I'm not getting him the juice," she told Sergeant Doty and headed to her own bedroom.

Across the room, Drake and Josh were talking to Sergeant Doty's partner, Officer McGraw.

"Isn't your dad the weather man on Channel 7?" he asked.

"Yeah, that's him," Josh answered.

"He said it wasn't going to rain on my kid's birthday," Officer McGraw said. "But it did rain."

"I'm sorry," Josh said, backing away.

Officer McGraw leaned in and narrowed his eyes. "Yeah. Me too."

Josh watched the officer walk back over to his partner, relieved that he wasn't going to get into any more trouble over his father's weather reports. The missing furniture was bad enough. He grabbed Drake's arm and pulled him across the room, away from the police.

"What?" Drake asked.

"We have to replace Mom and Dad's furniture," Josh said.

"Dude, do you know how much it's gonna cost to replace a whole room full of nice furniture?"

"A lot," Josh answered.

Drake patted his brother on the shoulder. "Well, good thing you have a job," he said, holding out his hand. "I'm gonna grab some tacos, give me twenty bucks."

Neither brother noticed Tyler peeking at them from behind the pass-through window, or the carton of eggs he placed on the counter.

"No!" Josh said in response to Drake's request for taco money. "Okay, my job at the Premiere doesn't pay me enough to refurnish this entire room. You and I are going to have to figure out how to make some money — fast."

Tyler picked up an egg, drew his arm back, and aimed over the brothers' heads for the police officers. It hit Sergeant Doty on the shoulder and broke, dripping down the back of his uniform.

The police officers turned around. Tyler had ducked back down behind the counter, so all they saw were Drake and Josh with an open carton of eggs behind them.

"Hey, you think eggs are funny?" Sergeant Doty yelled, walking toward them.

Drake and Josh froze.

"You know I could arrest the two of you for assaulting a police officer." He shook the egg off his hand.

"We didn't throw an egg at you," Drake said.

"We don't even have any eggs on us," Josh explained. He had no idea where the egg came from.

Officer Doty reached behind them for the carton of eggs. "Hah! Then whose are these?" he asked. "The egg fairy's?"

"We don't even know where those came from," Josh said.

"Fifty push ups," Sergeant Doty demanded.

Josh tried to reason with him. "You can't make us do push —"

"Push ups!" Sergeant Doty screamed, pointing to the floor.

Drake and Josh dropped to the floor and started counting. Megan watched it all from the hall. She caught Tyler's eye and nodded with a smile. He wasn't as good at pranking her brothers as she was, but he came pretty close.

CHAPTER SIX

By the next morning, Josh realized that the only way to make enough money to replace his parents' furniture was to get a temporary job — a high paying temporary job. He put on his best suit and tie and dragged Drake with him to the Fleeting Jobs agency. They filled out a form and sat in a waiting room. Josh practiced answering job interview questions while Drake slumped in his chair and tried to catch a few Z's. It was hard with Josh talking about his grade point average and his people skills the whole time.

Finally they heard their names called and they walked into a manager's office.

Josh walked in with a big smile, ready to demonstrate his firm handshake and his excellent people skills. Drake followed him.

"What do you want?" the manager asked. He looked bored out of his mind.

Drake dropped into one of the chairs in front of the manager's desk.

"We understand you give people temporary jobs," Josh said, sitting down. Clearly, this guy wasn't going to shake his hand.

"So?" the manager asked.

Josh looked at Drake. Was this guy serious, he wondered? "So, we'd like one," Josh said nervously.

The manager punched a few keys on his computer. "And I'd like to make a friend who doesn't change his phone number after the first time we hang out," he said dryly.

Drake totally understood why this guy had no friends. "Well, good luck with that," he said sarcastically.

Josh pressed his lips together, trying not to laugh.

"Okay, what are your skills?" the manager asked.

"I play guitar and date girls," Drake said.

The manager glared at him.

Josh jumped in to save the situation. If this guy didn't have friends, he didn't have dates either. Drake didn't need to point out the guy's shortcomings. Besides, Josh had been running over a list of his strengths and it was time to show off a little and get a really great, high-paying job. "Well, I'm an honor student," he said. "I'm pretty good with magic tricks. I can cook. Oh, and in the fifth grade I was voted most polite child —"

The interviewer cut him off with a loud groan. "Noooo," he screamed, throwing his hands up into the air. "That's enough."

Josh's draw dropped. Drake slumped down a little more in his chair. This guy was clearly on the edge, and they didn't want to do anything to set him off even more.

"Let's see," he said, adjusting his tie. "I've got men's room attendant, ditch digger."

The brothers looked at each other. When they said *job*, they hadn't meant anything gross or dirty.

"Or, you can clean up after elephants at the zoo."

"Wow, they all sound so wonderful," Drake said sarcastically.

"Do you have any jobs that are — you know — NOT repulsive," Josh asked.

"Yeah, and we want one that pays a lot," Drake explained.

"Sure," the manager mocked. "And I'd like to make a friend who doesn't change his phone number after the first time we hang out," he repeated.

Suddenly the guys figured it out. If their chances of getting a job that paid a lot were about the same as this guy's were at making and keeping friends, there was absolutely no chance that they'd get a job that paid a lot.

"You already said that," Josh pointed out.

"Well it happens every time!" the manager screamed. "What is wrong with me?"

Drake leaned back even farther into his chair and raised his hands in self-defense. He could tell there was a long list of things wrong with this guy, but that's not what he and Josh were there for. "We just want jobs," he said.

The manager adjusted his tie again and calmed down a little. He clicked some more keys on his computer. "All right, look, I've got two jobs working the line at a fish factory," he said, expecting the brothers to say no. "Not glamorous enough for you?"

"Well, what would we have to do?" Josh asked.

"You'd be assembling packages of sushi for distribution to local supermarkets," the man said, reading off his computer screen. "Pays eighteen bucks an hour — each."

The guys looked at each other. Eighteen bucks wasn't bad, and sushi wasn't nearly as repulsive as men's rooms and what came out of elephants.

"Yeah, we'll take it!" Josh said, answering for both of them.

"Good. Happy, happy," the manager drawled. His tone of voice and facial expression was the exact opposite of his words. "Here's the address," he said, jotting it down and ripping the page from his pad. "Be there Saturday morning. Eight o'clock."

Drake was totally shocked and disgusted. He had agreed to work a temporary job. He had even agreed to work in a fish factory. But Saturday mornings were for sleeping, not for working. Didn't this guy know that? "Eight o'clock?" he asked, his face screwed up in horror.

"We'll be there," Josh assured the manager.

"Yeah. Yeah," he said, waving Josh off.

The manager watched the brothers leave his office,

and then reached for the phone. He dialed his newest friend with a hopeful smile on his face. Maybe this would be the one. But instead of a person or an answering machine on the other end, he got the familiar voice recording from the phone company: "The number you have reached has been disconnected."

CHAPTER SEVEN

Saturday morning, Drake and Josh raced behind their new boss, a no-nonsense-looking woman named Irene, to their workstation at the Ball & Vance Fish Corporation. It was a small room, only big enough for two or three people. They stood behind a silver conveyor belt with small window openings at either end.

"All right, here is where we package the sushi," Irene said. She pointed to a light fixture over one of the small openings. "When that green light goes on, the sushi will move across the conveyor belt from here to there," she explained, waving her finger from one side of the conveyor belt to the other.

The guys looked at each other. Irene was talking at break-neck speed, but so far it seemed easy enough.

"Your job is to take the pieces of sushi off the conveyor belt and place them into these containers here." She pointed to a pile of black plastic boxes. "Then you place the containers back on the line there. Six pieces of sushi to one container.

"Now, if any sushi passes through there unboxed," she warned, pointing to the second window opening, "you will be fired, or forcibly escorted through that door there." Finally, she took a breath and her face cracked into something like a smile. "Any questions?"

Josh had one. "Yeah, is that —"

"I don't have time for questions," Irene spat, cutting him off. "Sit," she commanded.

Drake and Josh jumped onto the two stools behind the conveyor belt, and grabbed their paper chefs' hats.

"Let the sushi roll," Irene yelled to the next room.

Josh laughed. "I get it," he said, remembering that sushi is served in rolls. "Sushi roll."

But Irene didn't find anything about work funny. Work was serious. "That wasn't a joke," she said sternly. "That was an unfortunate coincidental pairing of words."

Josh wiped the smile off his face. *Okay*, he thought. No jokes here.

"Let the sushi roll," Irene yelled again, louder this time.

The guys heard a buzzer go off. The green light switched on and the conveyer belt started to move.

"I'll be back in two minutes to evaluate your performance," Irene said threateningly.

The guys each placed a black container in front of them and waited for the sushi to roll through the small window.

"Putting sushi in a box," Drake said, when Irene left the room. "How easy is this?"

"I know, right?" Josh agreed.

Drake spotted two pieces of sushi making their way through the opening. "And here we go," he said.

"Time to package some dead fish," Josh added.

They each reached for pieces of sushi. Josh whistled while he worked, filling one box and slipping it back onto the conveyor belt. He reached for another container.

Drake almost missed one piece, but saw it in time and popped it into his container, sending it on down the line. "Oh yeah," he said, "this is really challenging."

"All right. All right. It might not be the most exciting job in the world, but at least it will earn us enough money to get Mom and Dad some new furniture," Josh said. More sushi was coming through the opening now, and Josh had to speed up a little. He noticed one piece about to slip by Drake and through the opening at the other end. "Hey, grab that one," he warned.

"I got it. I got it. Don't worry," Drake said, reaching for it just in time. Then he grabbed another, and another. Both were about to slip through the opening.

The conveyor belt seemed to speed up. Josh grabbed two pieces of sushi in each hand. Drake didn't have time to grab a container, and was sliding sushi onto the ledge in front of him with one hand, while he fumbled for a box with the other.

"Whoa, this thing's going kind of fast," Josh said. He noticed that Drake was struggling too. "Hey," he shouted. "Can you slow it down a little bit?"

No one seemed to hear. The guys grabbed the sushi as fast as they could. Irene had been perfectly clear about what would happen if even one piece of sushi slipped through — they would be fired.

"Whoa. Whoa," Drake said, seeing that sushi was about to slip past him. "Grab more pieces."

"I'm grabbing. I'm grabbing," Josh said, moving as fast as he could. He dropped a handful of sushi on the side of the conveyor belt. "Put them on the side. Put them on the side," he told Drake.

"I'm trying," Drake said, but the belt was moving too fast.

There was no time to get all the sushi into containers. Josh desperately popped a couple of pieces into his mouth and started to chew. He had to destroy the evidence.

Drake swept a whole bunch of sushi off the belt and started slipping it down the front of his apron. Then he threw a piece up into the air. It hit the ceiling with a thwack and stayed there. "Dude, they stick," he said, pointing.

Desperately, the guys starting throwing sushi up into the air. Each time a piece hit the ceiling, it stuck.

Suddenly, the buzzer sounded again and the green light switched off. The belt stopped running.

"She's coming back," Drake yelled, eyeing all the sushi that was sitting in front of them. He threw another handful up to the ceiling and handed Josh his paper hat. Josh filled the hat with sushi while Drake hid some pieces under the stack of black containers. Finally, just as Irene was opening the door, Josh popped the last few pieces into his mouth.

Drake donned his now sushi-stuffed hat. It slipped down over his eyes, but to move it might mean that the sushi would fall out. He couldn't see and Josh couldn't talk, but between the two of them they had managed to hide all the sushi.

Irene didn't notice. Her eyes were on the conveyor belt. She saw that it was empty and nodded with satisfaction. "Excellent," she said. "You boys are doing a fine job."

Josh smiled, trying to hide the fact that he had a mouth full of sushi. Drake leaned nonchalantly against the conveyer belt, hoping his hat wouldn't fall off and give them away.

"Speed it up a little," Irene screamed, and then left the room.

The buzzer buzzed and the green light switched on.

Speed it up a little? Josh opened his mouth and let the sushi fall to the floor. The brothers eyed each other with frantic horror. There was no way they could keep up with this.

"Speed it up?" Josh yelled in frustration. He grabbed his hat and started filling it with sushi. "Oh, dude, grab it!"

"I'm trying. I'm trying," Drake said. He pulled his sneaker off and started filling it with fish. But the sushi was coming at them fast and furious now. He threw his shoe up into the air hoping it would stick. It didn't. It hit him in the head on the way down. "Oh," he groaned.

"I've got it. I've got it," Josh said, sweeping more pieces into his hat. For once he was glad he had a large head. "Ah, thank you. Thank you," he said to the hat, slapping it onto his head.

He and Drake frantically grabbed the sushi. They weren't even trying to put it into containers any more, they were just trying to keep it from slipping through the opening at the end of the conveyor belt.

"Thank you. All right. All right," Josh said, watching Drake fill his fists with tuna rolls. Then he grabbed a few pieces himself and threw them at the wall in frustration. "Will you slow it down?" he screamed through the window. "We're just boys."

But the sushi kept coming. They seemed to have moved from tuna rolls to California rolls.

"Grab them, Josh," Drake yelled suddenly.

Josh threw himself on the conveyor belt. "I'm trying," he said, but the sushi still kept coming. There was a never-ending supply of dead fish rolled in sticky rice and seaweed coming at them.

Drake tried to grab a piece as it slipped through the opening, but his arm went with it and he couldn't pull it back. "Help! Help me!" he yelled.

Josh grabbed Drake's other arm and pulled.

"Oh," Drake yelled, as his arm came free. He crawled up onto the conveyor belt, trying to grab all the sushi while Josh threw more pieces up into the air.

"Oh, dude!" Josh noticed that Drake was having a hard time staying put on the conveyor belt. "Don't go through the sushi hole!" he warned.

Drake slid off the belt and together the guys frantically threw sushi at the ceiling, but it turned out that the sushi wasn't as sticky as it seemed at first. Pieces of sushi hit Drake in the head. "They're falling down," he cried.

Josh got hit in the head too. "They're falling off the ceiling," he said.

"I know!" Drake screamed.

Josh popped a couple more pieces into his mouth while Drake kept throwing pieces at the ceiling. But it was too late — it was raining sushi. And it wasn't a gentle rain, it was a hailstorm. Any minute now, Irene would be coming in to forcibly escort them from the building.

A couple of hours later, the guys hobbled through their own front door.

Josh was so sore he could hardly move. "That was the worst day of my life," he said.

Drake couldn't stand his own scent. "I'm going to smell like dead fish for a week," he moaned.

"I've got yellowtail tuna under my finger nails," Josh said in disgust. He plopped onto the couch.

"Man, what is that in my pants?" Drake asked. "Feels like . . . spicy tuna." He slumped down next to Josh, then jumped up again. "Really spicy."

"Oh, man," Josh said, trying to keep his eyes open.

"What are we gonna do? I mean we can't just leave Mom and Dad's living room empty."

"Look man, we tried our best, okay?" Drake said. "I can't think of anything else —" he cut himself off when he realized he was sitting on a couch — Mom and Dad's couch! He pressed on the cushions to make sure the couch was real and not a dream.

Josh sat up. He looked down and moved from side to side. He was sitting on a couch! He looked around. All the other furniture was back too. "The furniture's back!" he yelled.

"We did it!" Drake said.

"We didn't do anything!" Josh said excitedly. But it was back — all of it.

Walter and Audrey Nichols walked into the room.

"Howdy boys," Mrs. Nichols said.

"Surprised?" Mr. Nichols asked them.

"Yeah! How'd you get our furniture back?" Josh asked.

"The police found the robbers' moving van," Mrs. Nichols explained.

"It was broken down about a half mile up the street," Mr. Nichols added.

Drake looked around again. He could hardly believe it. "And they found everything."

Mrs. Nichols nodded. "It's all here." Then she sniffed. "Hey, do I smell rotting sushi?"

"Yeah," Drake answered. "It's a long story."

"You see —" Josh said, trying to explain.

Mr. Nichols cut him off. He had listened to enough crazy schemes and explanations from the guys this week. He didn't have time to listen to another one "We don't want to know."

Mrs. Nichols looked up at him with a smile. "Yeah, we are going out to dinner to celebrate our anniversary."

"I'm taking her to the Petite Fromage," Mr. Nichols said. The Petite Fromage was a super-exclusive, super-expensive French restaurant.

"Oh, fancy," Drake said.

"I know," Mr. Nichols agreed. "The soup's thirty dollars." He turned to his wife with a smile. "C'mon, baby."

"Okay, baby," she answered.

But now Mr. Nichols was thinking about the bill. "Don't order the soup," he told her.

Josh watched them leave, then caught a whiff of his shirt. He sniffed the sleeve. Drake leaned in and smelled it too. "Oh man, you do reek," he said.

"Yeah, I know," Josh said, heading for the stairs. "I need a bubble bath."

"All right, that's cool." Drake followed him. "But don't take too long because I have to take a shower afterwards."

Just then they heard two high-pitched beeps. Suddenly, they found themselves caught up in a big fishing net and dangling from the ceiling.

"Hello!" Josh yelled. "Hello."

"Hey!" Drake screamed.

"We're in a net," Josh said, hoping that his mom and dad were still within hearing distance. They weren't. "Hey, what's going on?" he asked.

"I'll tell you what's going on," Drake spat. "It's that Tyler kid, Megan's assistant."

Megan came out of the kitchen, carrying a drink, with a big smile on her face. "Hey, idiots. How's it hanging?"

"Hey, tell your friend Tyler to cut us down," Josh demanded.

"Tyler didn't do this, I did," Megan said with a shrug. "I fired Tyler."

"Why?" Drake asked. "I thought you were too busy to prank us."

"Yeah," Megan agreed. "But letting someone else make your lives miserable doesn't give me that same warm feeling I get from doing it myself. So, I'll make time." She smiled at her brothers again before heading up the stairs. "Later," she yelled over her shoulder.

"Hey!" Drake yelled, watching her go.

"Megan, wait!" Josh pleaded.

"Megan, could you at least get us down from here?" Drake asked.

She peeked around the corner with a grin. "Sure," she said, pulling out a remote control device. She pressed a button and there were two more high-pitched beeps.

Drake and Josh hit the floor with a thud.

Part Two:
Josh Is Done

Prologue

Josh was completely stressed out. He sat at the dining room table with his chemistry book and his notes spread out around him. He nervously tapped his pencil on the table. "Oh man, Drake and I have this huge chemistry test tomorrow morning," he said.

Drake was totally relaxed. He hung out in his bedroom bouncing a Ping-Pong ball on a paddle. "Me and Josh have this insanely important chemistry test tomorrow," he said.

"So I've been studying all night, every night for a week," Josh announced.

"So I've been playing lots of Ping-Pong," Drake said. He picked up his cell phone and hit speed dial.

"Our teacher Mr. Roland is really tough," Josh sputtered nervously. "I mean if you're even one minute late to his class he's not gonna let —" Josh cut himself off when the phone rang. "Hello?" he said. It was Drake.

"Come upstairs and play Ping-Pong with me," Drake said.

Josh glared at the ceiling. "No. I'm studying and you should be *too*," he said.

"So Ping-Pong?" Drake asked again. Didn't Josh know by now that Drake didn't study?

"Noooooo!" Josh said, hanging up and getting back to his chemistry book. "Anyway, I've come up with a great way to remember the atomic weight of the elements. See, what I do —" He was cut off again by a ringing telephone. He didn't have to wait to hear who was calling — he knew it was Drake. "Yeah, what?" he spat into the phone.

"Where are you?" Drake asked.

Josh stared at the ceiling again, visibly frustrated. "Downstairs," he said.

"You said you were going to come up and play Ping-Pong," Drake said.

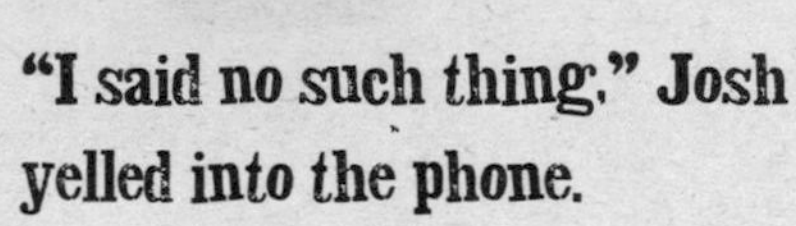

"I said no such thing," Josh yelled into the phone.

"So are you coming up?" Drake asked.

"No. I'm studying," Josh insisted.

But Drake just wouldn't take no for an answer. "Okay, I get first serve," he said.

"What is wrong with you?" Josh yelled into the phone. Then he hung up on Drake again. He was totally frustrated by Drake's refusal to understand that no means no. "I mean I do pretty well in chemistry, you know?" Josh explained. "But it's not like my strongest subject, and this test tomorrow counts for a huge percentage of our grade and —"

The phone rang again.
"Would you quit calling me,"
he yelled into the phone.

"Ping-Pong time!" Drake
sang into the phone.

"No!"

"C'mon," Drake wheedled.

Josh caved. "I get the good paddle," he said.

"You get the bad one," Drake answered.

Josh agreed reluctantly. He never got the good paddle. "Be right up," he said.

CHAPTER ONE

The next morning, Drake was wiping off the Ping-Pong table before school. Josh walked in, toweling his hair dry with one hand and holding his chemistry book in the other. He read out loud, trying to drill the information into his memory.

"Covalent bonds are composed of two electrons, one from each of the atoms. Carbon atoms can also form double bonds, which allow them —"

Drake interrupted with his new obsession. He waved a Ping-Pong paddle in the air. "Dude, c'mon, let's play."

"No," Josh said. "All right, I told you no Ping-Pong until I learn this —"

But Drake wasn't listening. He threw the paddle in Josh's direction, hitting him in the stomach.

"Ow! With which hand did you think I was going to catch that?" Josh asked sarcastically. Didn't Drake see that he had his hands full?

"C'mon man, quick game of twenty-one. You can serve," Drake urged.

"Dude, this chemistry exam counts for thirty percent of our grade," Josh said. "All right, you might not care, but I have to get an A."

"I care, sort of," Drake said, but then he got honest. He didn't care. "Not really." He waved a paddle in the air. "C'mon, let's play Ping-Pong."

"All right." Josh threw his towel and his chemistry book on his bed. There was no way Drake would let him study now anyway. "I'll play just to stop you from yapping."

"And the battle begins," Drake said in a deep voice. He sounded just like the voice over from a cheesy kung fu movie. He picked up a drumstick and banged it against a gong.

Josh crouched behind the Ping-Pong table and waved his paddle around.

"Oh, my worthy opponent," Drake said. "Are you prepared to Ping the Pong?"

"*Wah ha ha*," Josh said, in the same deep kung fu voice that Drake was using. "I am prepared, young

Sichuan. Your Pong is no match for my Ping." He made a figure eight in the air with his paddle.

Drake narrowed his eyes at him. "Do your worst," he intoned. Then he let out a high-pitched scream and served the ball to Josh.

The ball bounced back and forth, the brothers using their kung fu screams each time they returned the ball. Drake turned and hit the ball from behind his back. Josh raised his leg high and hit the ball from underneath his knee.

Josh reached his arm back, determined to make Drake miss a shot, and hit the ball hard. The paddle flew right out of his hand and out the window, breaking it with a loud crash.

Drake turned to look at the damage, then crouched behind the table again. "You have smashed the window of transparency," he growled.

Josh ran to the window. He could hear the neighbor's dog barking and hoped it hadn't been hit with a piece of flying glass. The dog was fine, but Josh was still in big trouble. "Oh man," he said in his own voice. "Mom and Dad are gonna kill me."

"Yeah, probably," Drake said nonchalantly. "C'mon lets finish the game."

"I don't have a paddle," Josh said, looking out the window. His paddle was smashed and lying in a puddle of broken glass.

"There's an extra one downstairs," Drake said. "Be back in a second."

"Look, we cannot be late for this test," Josh insisted.

Drake picked up the chemistry book and threw it to Josh. "It'll take ten seconds." "Here, study while I'm gone."

"I don't think that leaves us enough time —"

But Drake wasn't listening. He had already slammed the door and was halfway down the stairs.

Josh opened the book and used his kung fu voice to ask himself chemistry questions. "What is the atomic weight of beryllium?" he asked himself. "Nine point o one," he answered.

He checked the book. He was right! He let it be known by launching into a high-pitched kung fu scream.

* * *

Drake ran into the living room and grabbed a Ping-Pong paddle off the coffee table. He was on his way back upstairs when he heard a strange sound. It sounded like an elephant. An elephant with a stomachache. He peered into the kitchen and saw Megan sitting at the table with her laptop.

He heard the strange noise again. "What was that?" Drake asked.

Megan turned to look at him. "Humpback," she explained.

Drake did a double take. Was she insulting him? "Jerk," he responded.

Megan rolled her eyes with a sigh. "I wasn't calling you a name. That was the sound of a humpback whale."

"Oh," Drake said, suddenly understanding.

"Idiot," Megan said flatly. "*That* was me calling you a name," she explained with a smile.

"Yeah, well you know what?" Drake said, waving the Ping-Pong paddle at her. "I don't like you— "

He was interrupted by a ringing telephone. "Hello?" he said, breaking into a grin when he heard the voice on the other end. "Oh, hey Kat."

Megan clicked a button on her computer, and the sound of the humpback whale filled the kitchen.

Drake put his hand over the telephone receiver. "Hey, could you stop that, I'm trying to talk on the phone."

Megan looked at him and clicked the button again. The sound was even louder this time.

"Quit it," Drake snapped at her. Then he spoke into the phone. "No, sorry, it's just my little sister playing on her —"

Megan hit the button again.

Clearly Drake wasn't going to be able to hear Kat over the sounds of humpback whale songs. "I'll meet you by your locker in fifteen minutes," he said, and hung up. He turned to glare at Megan. "You know, when a pretty girl calls me and wants to talk before school, it doesn't help when you start blasting your whale sounds."

But Megan was unmoved. She simply clicked the button again and stared at Drake with a straight face.

"You're the worst," Drake said, grabbing his keys.

Megan laughed to herself as Drake slammed the front door behind him.

* * *

Josh ran down the stairs. Drake hadn't come back and it was time to leave for school. "Hey, hey, where's Drake?" he asked Megan, looking around.

"Do you think this whale sounds depressed?" Megan asked, playing the sound again.

"Where's Drake?" Josh shouted. He had no time for depressed whales. He checked his watch. "Our chemistry exam starts in less than a half an hour."

"He left," Megan said calmly.

"He left?" Josh screamed. "He did not leave." He ran through the living room, searching for Drake. Then he looked out the front door. The car they shared wasn't in the driveway. Josh slammed the door and headed back into the kitchen. "He left!" he shouted.

Megan laughed. "Yeah, I just said that."

"How can he just take the car and leave me stranded here?" Josh asked in a total panic. Their parents had already left for work, and Drake took the only other car. His mind raced. "Hey, when does your car pool get here? I need a ride to school."

"Ohhhh," Megan said, enjoying her brother's panic. "Bad news for you."

"What?" Josh asked.

"I'm not going to school. My class is going whale watching." She filled the kitchen with the songs of humpback whales again.

"Would you stop playing those songs?" Josh asked. He was starting to feel a little sick, and those noises weren't helping.

Megan simply hit the button again.

Josh shook his head. He should have known — the only way to make sure Megan did something was to let her know it was annoying. "Yeah, I didn't see that coming." He checked his watch again, trying to come up with a solution. "Okay, twenty-four minutes until I have to get to class. If I take my bike I should be able to get there in time." He ran toward the garage.

"You can't ride your bike," Megan yelled over her shoulder.

"Why?" Josh asked.

"Drake ran over it last night."

"Ohhhhhh," Josh screamed. He grabbed a spatula and started pounding it on the kitchen counter while he babbled nervously. "C'mon, that isn't fair, I mean, honestly!" He took a deep breath and tried to calm down. "Twenty-three minutes," he said checking his watch again. He paced back and forth, scratching his head. There had to be a logical solution. "Twenty-three minutes. Twenty-three minutes. Okay, twenty-three minutes until the exam starts. School's two and a half miles away. If I run at an average speed of seven and a half miles per hour . . ."

"Just go," Megan snapped. She was tired of hearing about his problems already.

Josh had already grabbed his backpack and was already half way to the door. "See ya!" His feet were moving as fast as they possibly could. "Feet don't fail me now!" he yelled.

CHAPTER TWO

Josh raced all the way to school, dashing across streets just as the light was about to turn from green to red, dodging around a group of old ladies on their morning walk, and leaping right over a kid on a tricycle. Between the panic and the running, he was a giant blob of sweat by the time he got to school.

The halls were practically empty when he arrived. He sprinted to the Science wing. He was going to make it by a tenth of a second.

The bell rang. Mr. Roland watched the second hand on the clock. When it reached eight o'clock, he addressed the students at the lab tables. "All right, class," he said. "Close your books. Put all materials underneath your desks." His eyes swept over the class. "Drake, stop whispering to Kat. Your exam is about to begin."

He closed and locked the classroom door. "You will have exactly fifty-five minutes to complete your —"

Just then, Josh banged into the door, running at full speed, and then bounced off it and onto the floor.

His sweaty hands left palm prints on the glass. "Please, please, let me in," he pleaded, banging on the door. "I'm sorry I'm late," he cried.

Mr. Roland opened the door and Josh burst through.

"Mr. Nichols, you know the rules," the teacher said firmly, standing in front of him.

"But you don't understand," Josh said. "See I was —"

But Mr. Roland understood all he needed to. "I understand that you are late. And when you're late to my class you're not welcome in my class."

"But what about the exam," Josh asked desperately. This exam was too important to miss!

"You will take a make-up exam next Saturday morning at six A.M., and you will be marked down one letter grade."

"Oh no," Josh groaned. He didn't know which was worse — having to take an exam at the crack of dawn, or losing a whole grade. He needed an A in this class! "No, no, no," he cried, shaking his head back and forth. This was awful. Then he spotted Drake — the reason why he was going to lose a letter grade on the chem test. "You," he said, pointing and narrowing his eyes. "You."

Drake blinked in confusion. "What?" he asked.

"Ahhhhh!" Josh took off on another run — straight for Drake, fists flying. He was going to kill him.

Had Josh finally cracked under the pressure of trying to get good grades, Drake wondered? He stepped behind a lab table for protection while two big guys grabbed Josh by the arms and held him until he calmed down a little.

"You will leave this classroom now!" Mr. Roland ordered.

Josh still hadn't given up completely. "But I —"

"Now."

"I just —"

"Now. Now. Now," the teacher repeated.

Josh tried to get back a little shred of his dignity. He adjusted the strap on his backpack. "Now?" he asked, totally defeated.

Mr. Roland pointed to the door. As soon as Josh stepped through it, Mr. Roland closed and locked the door behind him.

But Josh still wasn't ready to give up. He turned back to the window in the door. "Now if you would just allow me to explain," he pleaded.

But Mr. Roland pulled the shade and turned back to the class. "As I was saying, you will have fifty-five minutes to complete your exam. You will use a number-two pencil."

Josh had gone outside and made his way around to the classroom windows. His friends Craig and Eric tried not to look at him, standing there looking totally pathetic. But Josh wasn't done pleading.

"You are so hard," he cried, peering in the window at Mr. Roland.

Mr. Roland closed the blind.

Josh moved to the next window and finished his thought. "So unbelievably hard," he cried.

The next set of blinds closed in Josh's face. But there was still one window left.

"I want silence in this room," Mr. Roland said. He shut the last set of blinds while Josh continued to try to plead his case.

Josh was so upset he could barely form words. Everything came out in a wail.

Mr. Roland couldn't see Josh, but he could still hear him whimpering on the other side of the window. "Silence is golden," he said firmly.

By the end of the school day, Josh had calmed down and cleaned up. He sat on the couch in the living room in a sweat-free polo shirt, sipping lemonade and reading his chemistry book.

Megan breezed in from her field trip, carrying a big bag. "Hey."

"Hey, Megan. How was your whale watching trip?" Josh asked.

"Kind of fun," Megan answered. "The water was a little choppy, so Janie threw up on our teacher, which I enjoyed." She pulled a stuffed humpback whale out of her bag. "And look what I got at the souvenir shop." She squeezed the whale and it made those same awful sounds Josh had been forced to listen to that morning.

"Nice," Josh said, turning back to his book.

"And look," Megan said. "It's also an energy drink." She pushed a button and squirted liquid from the whale's blowhole into her mouth.

Josh watched her with a small smile on his lips. There was a time when he would have gotten excited about an energy-drink-producing whale. But not today. Not after this morning.

"How cute is that?" Megan asked with a giggle.

"Very cute," Josh agreed.

Megan headed into the kitchen, and Drake came in, slamming the front door behind him. Josh didn't look up. He didn't see Drake hide a giant green ball behind the couch.

"Hey, Josh, what goes on?" Drake asked smoothly.

"Just reading my book," Josh said quietly.

"Look, I'm sorry about this morning, all right?" Drake said. "But Kat called and wanted to talk before school. And you know . . . Kat," he added with a goofy smile on his face.

"Yes, she's very pretty," Josh said flatly.

"All right, you're still mad," Drake said. "But you won't be for long because I got you your very own . . ." Drake pulled the green ball out from behind the couch with a flourish ". . . sit and bounce." The ball had a handle on top, so a little kid could sit and bounce and hold on all at the same time.

Josh looked at it and then turned back to his book.

Drake put the ball behind his back and flourished it again. "Sit and bounce," he repeated.

"No thanks," Josh said.

Megan poked her head in from the kitchen. "Doesn't that kid Robbie next door have a sit and bounce just like that?"

Drake glared at her. "No," he said. She was going to totally ruin his "I'm sorry" gift. "Hey, c'mon," he said to Josh. "Have you ever sat and bounced before?" He sat on the ball and bounced up and down to demonstrate. "You can't be upset when you're sitting and bouncing."

Josh closed his book and stood. Clearly Drake wasn't going to give up. Josh was going to have to leave the room to get some studying done.

Drake bounced his way around the couch and right into Josh's path, springing up and down. He was sure that any minute now, Josh would forgive him and want to give the ball a try.

"Would you please move?" Josh asked quietly.

"C'mon, dude." Drake stopped bouncing and got serious. "I said I was sorry."

"I heard you," Josh said, walking past him.

"Then stop being mad at me," Drake said. It wasn't like Josh to hold a grudge. Usually Drake could expect him to scream and yell and then forgive him. That's what Drake wanted Josh to do now, but the weird thing was that Josh didn't seem mad — not anymore.

"I'm not mad at you," Josh said with a shrug. "I'm done."

Drake snorted. "Done? What is that supposed to mean?"

"I don't want anything to do with you anymore," Josh said.

"So what, are you going to move out?" Drake asked.

"No. This is the house where I live," Josh explained. "So I guess we'll be roommates until the day I leave for college. But that's all we'll be is roommates."

Drake's face fell. He had never heard Josh sound so serious and so sure.

"I'm done with you," Josh said again before heading upstairs to their room.

Even Megan was surprised. "Whoa," she said.

"What?" Drake asked her.

"You really did it this time," she said.

Drake wasn't ready to admit that. "Oh come on, you know how many times Josh has been 'furious' with me?" he said, putting air quotes around the word furious. "He'll pout for a day or two and then he'll get over it."

"I don't know, he sounded pretty serious," Megan said.

"Trust me," Drake assured her. "I know Josh and there's no way he's going to keep this whole —"

Robbie from next door chose that moment to slam through the front door. "I knew it!" he shouted when he spotted his sit and bounce. He marched across the living room. "I knew you took my sit and bounce." He kicked Drake in the shin, grabbed his toy, and bounced back out again.

CHAPTER THREE

A few days later, Josh hung out at the Premiere with his friends Craig and Eric, and his co-worker Leah. They were laughing over one of Eric's stories.

"So me and Craig are in the swimming pool, right?" Eric laughed. "Halfway through a game of Marco Polo."

"This is so great," Craig said.

"I look down and realize, he's still got his socks on!" Eric said.

The group cracked up. This was Eric's third story about Craig's goofy fashion mistakes.

"Argyle," Craig added, laughing at himself along with the others.

"He forgot to take them off!" Eric explained.

"No way!" Leah said.

"True story," Craig assured her.

"You know that same thing happened to me once, too," Josh said. "I was at canoe camp and my boat buddy was from Indonesia, right?"

Crazy Steve, another of Josh's co-workers, interrupted. "Excuse me, Josh? I'm having a little problem with the popcorn machine," he said. "Would you mind giving me a hand?"

Josh had been working at the Premiere for so long that he was an expert at getting the popcorn machine to work. But didn't Steve see that Josh was hanging with his friends, and that he wasn't wearing his uniform?

"Well, I'm not working tonight," Josh explained. "So could you ask someone else?"

Now here's the thing about Crazy Steve. He earned his nickname because he was totally crazy. Josh had seen him wig out over the silliest things. And Josh's refusal to jump in and get his hands full of popcorn grease was one of those things. "Sure!" Steve screamed right into Josh's face. Then he grabbed Craig's hot dog out of its bun and threw it across the room.

Then he leaned into Josh's face again, screaming. "Thanks for nothing!"

"What's the matter with him?" Eric asked.

"Why'd he chuck my wiener?" Craig said, staring down at his empty bun.

Drake missed the whole fiasco. "What's up, people?" he asked, grabbing a chair and joining the group.

"Hey, Drake," Leah said.

Josh didn't say a word.

Drake tried to pretend that things were normal between them. "So, Josh, tonight I'm thinking we either see *She's the Dude* or *Just My Truck*," Drake said.

"I heard both those movies were awful," Leah told him.

"Yeah, that's the point," Drake explained to her. "You see the first Tuesday of every month Josh and I see the worst movie out there. We call it bad movie Tuesday." He turned to Josh. "So which one do you want to see."

"Actually, we're going to see a laser light show downtown," Josh said.

"Oh, yeah." Eric checked the clock. "We'd better get going."

Drake watched the group get up to leave. He grabbed Josh's arm and held him back for a minute. "Dude, it's been like five days. When are you going to stop being mad at me?"

"I told you I'm not mad at you," Josh said patiently. "I'm done with you."

"Josh," Drake said, trying to cajole him into forgiveness.

"I mean it," Josh said over his shoulder.

Drake watched Josh walk away. His stomach dropped. Could Josh really be serious this time? Was he really done with Drake?

Saturday afternoon, Drake sat on his bed wrapped in a quilt and tried to tune his electric guitar. He tightened a string.

"No," he said to himself. "It's still flat." He picked up Megan's new stuffed whale and squeezed some energy juice into his mouth before slamming the toy back down onto his loft bed. The room momentarily filled with humpback whale songs.

Drake leaned back with another big sigh, and strummed his guitar. It was still off-key. "Come on!" he moaned.

Megan stormed in, her brown eyes flashing. "Did you take my whale?" she demanded.

"I was thirsty," Drake said, wondering why Megan was making such a big deal over a stuffed animal.

"I don't want you drinking from my whale without asking me," Megan said, snatching the whale off his bed.

"I'm sorry," Drake said.

"And have you even gotten out of bed today?"

"Go play with your whale," Drake spat with an injured expression. So he had stayed in bed all day. It's not like he had anything better to do.

"Oh, I guess someone's a little upset he doesn't have a brother anymore," Megan said.

"You know, if Josh doesn't want me in his life, fine with me," Drake said.

"Is it?" Megan asked knowingly.

"Yes," Drake insisted.

"Is it?" Megan asked again.

"Yes!" Drake repeated, more emphatically. "And let me tell you a little something, all right. He needs me way more than I need him."

Megan didn't believe him. "You think?"

"C'mon, without me Josh's life would totally fall apart," Drake said.

"I don't know." Megan held her whale up in front of her face. "What do you think about that, whale?" she asked, giving him a squeeze. His lonely song filled the room. "Whale's not so sure," Megan said, turning back to Drake.

"Yeah, well why don't you take your little whale and go play in the —"

"Hey, Megan," Josh said, coming into the room.

"Hey," Megan answered.

"You know that chemistry exam I had to make up this morning?" Josh asked her with her huge smile.

"Yeah."

"Aced it!" Josh announced proudly. "Didn't miss a single question. Mr. Roland was so impressed he's not going to even knock off a letter grade. That means I got a one hundred percent, baby!" He raised his hand for a high five. "Up top!"

Megan simply stared at him. She didn't do high fives with geek brothers.

But Josh was too happy to care; he kept babbling to Megan while he looked for something in his closet. He didn't even seem to notice that Drake was in the room. "Oh, you know that cute check-out girl at the Stop and Shop? She asked me out on a date."

Megan laughed. "She's like eighty years old."

Josh's face fell. "Not the express line. Register five."

"Oh," Megan said. Register five wasn't so cute either, but she decided not to rub it in.

"And now," Josh said, putting on his shades and grabbing a racquet, "I'm off to the gym to play me a little racquet ball with Helen."

"Your boss?" Megan asked. Josh sounded way too excited to be on his way to see the manager of the Premiere. Helen hated Josh. She was just as likely to use Josh's head as the ball as play a game with him.

"Yeah, we've been getting along a lot better lately," Josh said with a smile. "See ya, Megs!"

Megan watched Josh run down the stairs, then turned to the brother who didn't seem to be able to get out of bed. "Doesn't seem to me like his life is falling apart," she said.

"You just wait, all right," Drake assured her. "Without me, Josh's life is nothing."

Megan gave her whale another squeeze and left the room.

Drake went back to tuning his guitar. It still didn't sound right, and then a string broke with a loud twang. He slumped back against his bed and closed his eyes.

CHAPTER FOUR

Josh had to work Saturday night. He stood behind the snack counter at the Premiere and handed a woman a tub of popcorn. "You enjoy your popcorn," he said with a smile.

The woman smiled back and handed him a ten-dollar bill. "And you, keep the change."

"Wow, a six dollar tip," Josh said. "That's so nice. Thanks."

"You're very welcome," the woman said, and headed into her movie.

Josh pocketed his tip and headed over to the café tables with a rag and table cleaner.

His friends Craig and Eric walked in. That's why Josh liked working at the Premiere — most of his friends hung out there.

"Hey, Josh," Eric said. "You left your rash cream in my glove compartment." Eric knew all about Josh's rash. In fact, everyone knew about Josh's rash. He'd had it for years.

"Keep it," Josh said with a satisfied nod.

"Huh?" Eric asked.

"My rash went away," Josh said. He sprayed and wiped a table.

"You've had that rash for three years," Craig said.

"Why would it just go away all of a sudden?" Eric asked.

"I'm not sure," Josh said with a shrug. "Doctor Fishbaum says it could have been stress related."

"Ah," Craig said with a nod.

"Wait, when did you first notice it was gone?" Eric asked.

Josh squirted cleaner on another table. "About a week ago," he said.

"So just about the time you kicked Drake out of your life?" Eric asked.

Josh nodded. "Yeah," he said, heading back to the snack counter.

Crazy Steve leaned on the counter. "So how was your racquet ball game with Helen?" he asked Josh.

Josh was always a little afraid to talk to Steve. You never knew when he was going to wig out. He waited for a second before answering. "Awesome. I beat her two games out of three."

Leah had overheard from her post at the ticket window. She looked over, totally surprised. "You beat Helen?" she asked.

"She's like the pro," Steve said.

"I know," Josh said, slipping his hands into his pockets. "I was just on fire."

"Fire!" Crazy Steve screamed at the top of his lungs. He lunged for the cleaning spray and sprayed it into his own face.

"No! No! There's no fire," Josh yelled, getting a face-full of cleaning solution himself when he tried to take the bottle away. "Take a breath," he said, rubbing Steve's head. "In and out. In and out."

Crazy Steve calmed down.

"All right," Josh said, letting go of him.

Steve hugged the cash register, totally relieved to be burn free, and Josh reminded himself — again — to choose his words very carefully whenever Steve was within earshot. But he only had a moment, because Drake stormed into the Premiere.

"Hello, Josh," he said in a loud, angry tone of voice.

"Hello, Drake," Josh said quietly.

Craig and Eric watched from the other side of the café. "Why are you all sweaty?" Craig asked.

Drake glared at his brother. "I'm all sweaty because I ran out of gas and I had to walk all the way here because somebody forgot to fill up the car," he yelled.

"It's not my responsibility to fill the car with gas," Josh said, in the same quiet tone of voice.

"You always fill up the car!"

"Used to," Josh said with a shrug. He was done with funding Drake's driving. "Now I put in just enough gas for myself."

Drake was so frustrated he could hardly speak. And he certainly didn't have a comeback. The fact was, Josh had been paying for Drake's gas ever since they got their driver's licenses. "Well good. Good for you," Drake shouted. "I don't need your gas."

Josh didn't react.

"And just so you know," Drake's voice rose in frustration. "I'm going to see a movie right now, and I don't need a free ticket from you because

Mom gave me ten bucks to get out of the house." He pointed at Josh for emphasis. "So I don't need you for anything."

He stormed toward the ticket window.

"Movie tickets here are eleven dollars," Leah pointed out.

"What?" Drake asked.

"And popcorn and soda are going to cost you another six or seven," Eric said.

"Ohhhh," Drake screamed, his face screwed up in total exasperation. "You know what?" he said to Josh. "I'm not even going to buy a ticket. I'm just going in." He marched toward the door of theater seven. "I'm just going right in," he shouted, pushing past the usher at the door.

Josh cleared his throat and calmly picked up a walkie-talkie. "Security," he said. "We have a problem in theater seven. Male, Caucasian, sweaty, wearing a gray sweatshirt." He signed off and turned to Steve and Leah. "So what's the difference between a hoagie and a submarine sandwich?" he asked.

"I always thought a hoagie was a hot sandwich,"

Steve answered. "And a submarine could be served hot or cold.

"No, I think it's the other way around," Craig said.

That raised another question. "What's a grinder?" Eric asked.

"Same thing as a hoagie," Leah said.

The group was still talking about sandwiches when two big security guards walked past, dragging Drake between them.

"Hey! Let go. Let go!" Drake yelled. "Josh, tell them to let me go. Josh! Josh! Tell them," Drake screamed.

Josh said nothing, and the security guards continued to pull Drake through the lobby.

"Wait, I know this guy. Ask him," he said, pointing to Josh.

The guards stopped for a second. "Is this guy a friend of yours?" one of them asked.

Josh stared at Drake. His facial expression didn't change. "No he's not," Josh said seriously.

"Josh!" Drake said.

But Josh didn't say another word and the guards picked Drake up again and started hauling him toward the door.

"You're going to regret this, Josh," Drake screamed, frantically kicking his legs in the air. "You need me! You need me!"

Josh still didn't react. He watched the guards throw Drake out of the front door and turned to his friends. "So a hoagie and a grinder are the same thing, huh?" he asked.

CHAPTER FIVE

Josh sat at his lab table in chemistry class Monday morning. The bell rang indicating that class was about to begin. Mr. Roland kept an eye on the second hand on the clock.

"Students, class will begin in exactly nine seconds," he said, moving toward the door. "Please prepare yourselves."

Mr. Roland closed the door and was about to lock it when Drake burst in. "I'm here," he said, totally out of breath. "I'm here."

"Yes, with three seconds to spare," Mr. Roland said.

"Sorry, it's just that Josh used to wake me up every morning." Drake glared at his brother.

"Used to," Josh said.

"Mr. Parker, your personal problems don't interest me," Mr. Roland said. "Please go to your lab station."

"Yes, sir," Drake said, heading to the lab table he had been sharing with Josh all year. "Hi, Kat," he said, walking past her.

"Hi, Drake." She took a closer look at his chin. "Is that a zit?"

Drake stopped short. "Huh?"

Kat handed him a mirror and Drake took a look. "Oh no!" he said. "I've never had a zit before. I'm Drake. I don't get zits."

"Drake, please," Mr. Roland said. He couldn't start class until Drake took his seat and stopped talking.

"Why do I have a zit?" Drake asked.

"Just sit down," Mr. Roland said.

Drake simply stared at him, totally overcome by the idea of a zit.

"Sit," Mr. Roland repeated. "Sit down at your lab station."

Drake finally headed to his seat, but someone else was already in it. "Move!" Drake demanded.

"Roki is my new lab partner," Josh explained.

"Dude, I'm your lab partner," Drake insisted. "I've been your lab partner all year."

Josh spoke very slowly, as if he was talking to a toddler. "I asked Mr. Roland if I could switch, and now Roki is my new lab partner."

Drake stared at him, too shocked to speak.

"I realize this is awkward," Roki said, slipping on his safety goggles.

"Well who's gonna be my lab partner now?" Drake asked Mr. Roland.

Mr. Roland looked around the room. "You will work with Clayton," he said, spotting an empty seat at a lab station.

Clayton? Drake thought.

A guy with bright red hair, super thick glasses, and a goofy smile turned and waved from the front row.

"Oh, no!" Drake said heading for the empty seat. Clayton was the weirdest kid in school. He was such a dork that even the dorks avoided him. And he mumbled in such a strange, high-pitched voice that he sounded more like one of Megan's humpback whales than a person.

"Hi, Clayton," Drake said reluctantly.

"Hi," Clayton squeaked back.

"All right, your instructions are on the board," Mr. Clayton said. "Please begin your experiments."

Drake looked around. Kids were slipping on their safety goggles and picking up beakers of green liquid. Drake slid on his goggles and looked over his shoulder at Josh. Josh was already working, making whatever chemical concoction they were supposed to create.

There was a container of white powder in front of Drake. He picked it up and turned to Clayton. "What am I supposed to mix this stuff with?"

Clayton said something completely unintelligible and handed Drake a beaker with clear liquid.

"What?"

Clayton went off again, but Drake couldn't make out any words.

"I don't know what you're saying," Drake said, totally frustrated.

Eric was sitting just across the aisle. "Drake, you'd better hurry or Mr. Roland's going to get mad."

"Well I don't know what to do," Drake said. "Josh usually does everything and I just watch."

Eric started to explain. "Just take the magnesium sulfate —"

"No talking," Mr. Roland announced, cutting him off.

Eric shrugged and turned away.

Drake watched Clayton stirring something in a glass. He picked up the two beakers in front of him and started to add the white powder to the clear liquid. The liquid turned green and started to foam. It quickly spilled over the top of the beaker and all over Drake's hand.

"Whoa! Hey, what's happening?" he asked.

Clayton jumped back.

"What's happening?" Drake yelled. "Okay. Arm's tingling. Arm's tingling."

Craig noticed from across the room. "Chemical emergency!" He jumped to push an alarm button on the wall. A red light started to blink and a siren went off.

"Let's get him to the power shower," Mr. Roland said, picking up Drake and bringing him to a shower stall in the back of the room.

Roki closed and locked the shower door.

"Hey, hey, watch it! What is this?" Drake asked.

Mr. Roland pulled a cord.

"What are you —" Drake's question was cut off by his own scream when hot water started to pour over him.

"Drake, are you all right?" Mr. Roland asked.

But Drake couldn't answer — all he could do was scream. The shower was too small for him to get out of the range of the hot water. He finally realized that he should make sure his arms were cleaned of the chemicals.

Mr. Roland cut the water off. "Drake, you may come out now."

Drake stumbled out of the shower and took his goggles off, rubbing his eyes.

"Sit down, Drake," Mr. Roland told him.

But Drake rushed toward the front of the room.

"Drake, sit down," Mr. Roland said again.

"No," Drake shouted. He was too angry and embarrassed to sit. All he wanted to do was get out of there. He almost slipped and fell and he reached for the door handle, and then suddenly, Drake knew what he had to do. He turned and faced his brother. "Josh!" he yelled.

Josh had been concerned about Drake a minute ago, but now he was mad. He was always cleaning up Drake's messes, and he was sure Drake was going to try and make him do that once again. "What?" Josh yelled back at him.

"Look, I'm sorry," Drake said.

Josh blinked in surprise. "Well —"

"Let me finish, okay. I was wrong, okay? I was wrong," Drake said.

"What do you mean?" Josh asked.

"I need you more than you need me," Drake admitted. "I need you *way* more than you need me, all right? I'm sorry. Man, I'm sorry I made you late for your exam, and I'm sorry I ran over your bike, and I'm sorry I'm probably the worst brother in the world, and you're way better off without me, you know?"

Josh was speechless. He had never seen Drake so upset.

"I just need you to understand that I . . . I just . . ." Drake looked around the room, trying to come up with words that would make this right, but there was nothing. He realized that Josh really was better off without him, and the best thing Drake could do was stay out of his way. "I'm sorry, man. I'm sorry," Drake repeated. Then he ran out of the room.

Even Mr. Roland's hard heart was touched by Drake's apology. "Josh, would you like to go talk to Drake?" he asked gently.

But Josh had been through this too many times. He couldn't clean up any more of Drake's messes. He couldn't be the geek to Drake's cool guy image. His life was better without Drake in it, wasn't it? "No, sir," he said.

"All right, class, let's get back to our experiments," he announced and walked to the front of the room.

Josh stared at the beaker in front of him, but all he could see was Drake's hurt face.

CHAPTER SIX

Megan came home from school that afternoon to find Drake curled up on his Ping-Pong table wearing an old pair of cowboy pajama bottoms and a T-shirt. He was using a Ping-Pong paddle as a pillow and sadly bouncing a ball up and down.

"Hey, here's your guitar," Megan said.

"Thanks," Drake mumbled.

"You're not even going to ask me why I took your guitar?" Megan asked.

"Why'd you take my guitar?" Drake asked.

"I used it to kill a spider," Megan said with a satisfied smile.

Drake didn't yell and scream at her. He didn't even speak.

"Okay, why aren't you freaking out?" Megan asked. "It's not fun messing with you if you're not going to freak out."

"I'm sorry," Drake said.

"Okay," Megan said, clearly disappointed.

Drake tried to keep her in the room. "Hey, want to play some Ping-Pong?"

"No. You really don't want to put a paddle in my hand." Megan laughed and headed out of the room. "Later."

Drake hadn't played Ping-Pong in more than a week. Since the morning of his chemistry test. He bounced a ball on the table and then hit it across. There was no one on the other side to hit it back. Then he hit another. But they just bounced off the other end. The second paddle laid there, unused.

Josh had been thinking about his brother all day. He knew it took a lot for Drake to admit that he needed Josh, and especially that he needed Josh more than Josh needed him. Now Josh wondered was his life really better off without Drake? Sure, he was acing tests and playing the best racquetball ever, but that was mostly because he had a lot more time to study and practice.

He didn't have to clean up Drake's messes and he didn't have to keep filling the car with gas that Drake used up, but there was definitely something missing.

Josh hadn't laughed nearly as much this week as he did when he hung out with Drake. He missed things like all-night Ping-Pong marathons, and bad movie Tuesdays. He remembered how Drake helped Josh pretend he could sing and play the guitar to get the attention of a girl Josh liked, and how Drake was Josh's biggest supporter when Josh entered the science fair — even though Drake thought it was geeky. And who else would stand on line with Josh for hours just to ride a roller coaster on opening day, or sit through one more of Josh's magic shows?

Maybe Drake did need Josh more than Josh needed Drake, but that didn't mean Josh didn't need Drake at all. Josh had more fun with Drake than he ever had with anyone else. Suddenly, Josh realized that the best thing that had ever happened to him was becoming Drake's stepbrother.

He stood outside their bedroom listening to Drake play Ping-Pong by himself, and Josh knew what he had to do.

He jumped into the room and crouched like he was ready for battle. Raising his arms as if he was ready to strike, Josh let out a howl in his kung fu voice. "*Wah ha.* We have unfinished business, young Sichuan," he said.

Drake looked up, surprised and grateful. "Josh," he said seriously.

But this wasn't the time for more apologies. Josh cut him off with another war cry. "You can address me only as Master Moncoco."

The brothers smiled at each other.

"Your words, they are strong," Drake replied in a deep voice, "but your skills are weak."

"Your foolishness, young Sichuan, has sealed your fate," Josh told him. He raised his paddle, ready to go to battle.

"Oh, destiny is mine," Drake growled. He served the ball.

The guys — brothers and best friends again — let out a series of high pitched battle cries as they hit the ball back and forth. This was one game where the final score wouldn't matter. They were both winners.